Mummy Goes To Work

JOANNA LAMBERT

Essex, England
2020

Mummy wakes up early and grabs her bag and coat.

On her way to her job,
she always leaves a note.

Mummy goes to work each day, her job is in the city.

She works until the sun goes down and the stars look so pretty.

We asked our mummy, "Why do you work? It always makes you sigh."

She said,
"I do it all for
you. Now let me
tell you why."

Mummy works long hours to earn us lots of money,

so we can have a big,
big dog and a fluffy
bunny.

Mummy looks so tired
when she picks you up
at school,

but takes you to your football club

and the swimming pool.

Mummy comes home late sometimes but picks up all your toys.

Listens to you playing games and making lots of noise.

Mummy's home when
you feel ill, she wipes
your little nose,

cleans up all your tissues and washes all your clothes.

Mummy sometimes needs to rest but sits with you to play.

She cooks a lovely dinner for you,

every single day.

Mummy's shoes hurt her feet and make her toes so red.

Yet she walks you up the stairs, when it's time for bed.

Mummy gets some time off work, so takes you to the park

to ride your bike

and feed the ducks, before it gets too dark.

Mummy doesn't get much sleep but she's always there each night,

to read a book, kiss
your head

and tuck you in so tight.

We want to thank you mummy, for everything you do,

so we give you lots of
hugs and tell you,

"We love you!"

THE END

Printed in Great Britain
by Amazon

40436489R00018